Bedtime for Bear

Anne Phillips
Illustrated by David McPhail

RIGBY

Yawn!
I want to
sleep.

Whooo!
Whooo!
Shhh!
I want to
sleep.

Chirp! Chirp!
Shhh! I want to sleep.

Squeak! Squeak!
Shhh! I want to sleep.

Ribbit! Ribbit!
Shhh! I want to sleep.

zzzzzzzZ

Shhh!
We want to sleep!
zzzzzzzz